W9-CAF-636

West Chicago Public Library District
118 West Washington
West Chicago, IL 60185-2803
Phone # (630) 231-1552
Fax # (630) 231-1709

Pinkalicious ™

Tickled Pink

by Victoria Kann

HARPER FESTIVAL
An Imprint of HarperCollinsPublishers

For Margaret, Michael, Wes, and Carly,
you tickle me pink!
—V.K.

The author gratefully acknowledges
the artistic and editorial contributions
of Bob Masheris and Natalie Engel.

HarperFestival is an imprint of HarperCollins Publishers.

Pinkalicious: Tickled Pink
Copyright © 2010 by Victoria Kann

Based on the HarperCollins book *Pinkalicious* written by
Victoria Kann and Elizabeth Kann, illustrated by Victoria Kann

Library of Congress catalog card number: 2010923263
ISBN 978-0-06-192877-2

Book design by John Sazaklis
10 11 12 13   CWM   10 9 8 7
❖
First Edition

I was in the library, looking for a good book.

giggle giggle

ha ha ha ha

I poked around the shelves until I found something
with a bright pink cover and shiny gold letters.
   The Goofy Book of Gags and Giggles, I read.
I opened it up.

It was full of hilarious jokes! I started reading and giggling. I bit my lip to try to keep from laughing out loud, but the jokes were too funny.

I checked the book out and put it in my backpack until recess.

giggle   ha ha

ha ha

The Goofy Book of
Gags
and
Giggles

giggle giggle

When it was finally time to go outside, I took the book with me.

"What are you reading, Pinkalicious?" Molly asked.

"A joke book I found," I said. "Listen to this:
Where do cows go on a first date?
To the MOOvies!"

Molly couldn't stop laughing. We laughed so hard that Alex and Alison came over to see what was going on.

"Pinkalicious has a joke book," said Molly. "Go ahead, Pinkalicious, read them another one."

"Okay," I said. "Why do birds fly south in the winter?"

"Why?" said Alex, Molly, and Alison.

"Because it's too far to walk!" I said.

We giggled until our tummies hurt. I told them another joke and another. Soon everyone was listening to us.

"Pinkalicious, you're hilarious!" one kid said, laughing.

"No she's not," said Tiffany, who was listening the whole time. "Anyone can be funny if they're reading from a book. I bet Pinkalicious doesn't have a real funny bone in her body."

"I do, too!" I shouted, my cheeks turning pink with anger.

"Prove it," said Tiffany. She challenged me to a laugh-off for the next day.

"You can tell any joke you want, but you have to make it up yourself," she said.

I wasn't sure I could think of a joke as good as the ones in my book, but I agreed. Everyone was watching. What else could I do?

That night, I told my family about my dilemma.
"I need to create a joke that's fizzier than pink lemonade, more fun than pink cupcakes, more pinkatastic than pink!" I said. "It has to be the most pinkerrifically funny joke of all time."

"Hey, Pinkalicious. I have a joke," said Peter. "Knock, knock."

"Who's there?"

"Pinky, stinky underwear!" Peter practically laughed himself right off his chair.

"Yuck, Peter," I said. "NOT funny. Not funny at all."

I paced and pouted and panicked. I had to remind myself to calm down.

"Think pink," I said, "and the answer will follow."

In the middle of the night, I had an idea. Maybe, just maybe, it would be good enough to win.

The next morning, I had trouble swallowing my cereal. My stomach felt funny all during school. Then, at last, the big moment came.

"It's time for the laugh-off," yelled Alex. "First up is Tiffany."

Tiffany strutted up to the jungle gym.

"What's black and white and red all over?" she said.

"An embarrassed zebra?" someone said.
"No," Tiffany said.
"A sunburned skunk?"
"No."
"What?"
"A PENGUIN WHO ATE ALL THE PINK CUPCAKES!"
Everybody laughed. I was going to lose, big time.

I was next, and I was worried. My joke had seemed funny in the middle of the night, but it didn't seem all that funny now. *What if nobody gets it? What if nobody laughs?* I thought.

"What's the matter, Pinkalicious?" yelled Tiffany. "Can't you be funny without your book?"

I walked over to the jungle gym. I looked at all the kids looking at me. My mouth felt dry. I swallowed. *Oh well,* I thought, *even if my joke isn't the best, at least everyone will know it's my own.*

"What's even funnier than being tickled?" I said.

"BEING TICKLED PINK!" I cried. I tickled people until they laughed so hard their faces turned bright pink. Everyone was laughing—even Tiffany.

"Okay, Pinkalicious," she said. "I guess you do have a funny bone after all."

"Thanks." I smiled with relief. "I liked your joke, too."

After the laugh-off, I returned the joke book to the library. Now that it was over, nothing seemed quite as funny as being tickled pink!